P9-DNA-449

GET A CLUE

OPERATION
YELLOW DRAGON
A PICTURE MYSTERY

DISCARDED

WAYNE PUBLIC LIBRARY

SEP 1 9 2008

GET A CLUE

OPERATION
YELLOW DRAGON
A PICTURE MYSTERY

Julian Press

GROSSET & DUNLAP

GROSSET & DUNLAP

Published by the Penguin Group

Penguin Group (USA) Inc., 375 Hudson Street, New York, New York 10014, USA

Penguin Group (Canada), 90 Eglinton Avenue East, Suite 700, Toronto, Ontario M4P 2Y3, Canada

(a division of Pearson Penguin Canada Inc.)

Penguin Books Ltd., 80 Strand, London WC2R 0RL, England

Penguin Group Ireland, 25 St. Stephen's Green, Dublin 2, Ireland

(a division of Penguin Books Ltd.)

Penguin Group (Australia), 250 Camberwell Road, Camberwell, Victoria 3124, Australia

(a division of Pearson Australia Group Pty. Ltd.)

Penguin Books India Pvt. Ltd., 11 Community Centre, Panchsheel Park, New Delhi—110 017, India

Penguin Group (NZ), 67 Apollo Drive, Rosedale, North Shore 0632, New Zealand

(a division of Pearson New Zealand Ltd.)

Penguin Books (South Africa) (Pty.) Ltd., 24 Sturdee Avenue,

Rosebank, Johannesburg 2196, South Africa

Penguin Books Ltd., Registered Offices: 80 Strand, London WC2R 0RL, England

If you purchased this book without a cover, you should be aware that this book is stolen property.
It was reported as "unsold and destroyed" to the publisher, and neither the author
nor the publisher has received any payment for this "stripped book."

The scanning, uploading, and distribution of this book via the Internet or via any other
means without the permission of the publisher is illegal and punishable by law.
Please purchase only authorized electronic editions and do not participate in or encourage
electronic piracy of copyrighted materials. Your support of the author's rights is appreciated.

Copyright © 2006 by cbj Verlag, a division of Verlagsgrupped Random House GmbH, Munchen, Germany.
Translated and adapted by the Miller Literary Agency, LLC. All rights reserved.
Cover background copyright © Mayang Murni Adnin, 2001-2006.
Published by Grosset & Dunlap in 2008, a division of Penguin Young Readers Group,
345 Hudson Street, New York, New York 10014.
GROSSET & DUNLAP is a trademark of Penguin Group (USA) Inc.
Printed in the U.S.A.

Library of Congress Cataloging-in-Publication Data is available.

ISBN 978-0-448-44875-6   10 9 8 7 6 5 4 3 2 1

INTRODUCTION

The Sugar Shack sold the best candy in Hillsdale, the tiny town where best friends Josh, David, and Lily lived. The Sugar Shack was owned by Lily Shipman's uncle, Frank. Lily, David, and Josh spent a lot of time there after school. Sometimes Lily's other uncle, Tony, dropped by. Tony was a police detective and a sucker for lollipops. The three friends loved mysteries, suspense stories, and solving puzzles, so they constantly harassed Tony with questions about his work. One day Tony suggested they start up their own detective agency. They could use the candy storage room in the attic of the Sugar Shack as their headquarters, and Frank and Tony could be their technical consultants. The three friends jumped at the chance! It was no time at all before they solved their very first case . . .

MEET THE DETECTIVES

 Frank Shipman is friendly and always in a good mood. He loves to solve crossword puzzles.

 Inspector Tony Shipman is a night owl. When the rest of the world is asleep, he's always hard at work at his computer, solving cases.

 Josh Rigby, the youngest detective in the group, has a sharp eye and an even sharper wit. A do-it-yourself genius, he's never short of ideas.

 David Doyle loves nature and the outdoors. He can make all different kinds of birdcalls. His cockatoo follows him everywhere.

 Lily Shipman thinks faster than lightning, and playing sports has given her a real sense of how to work as a team.

 Robinson, David's beloved cockatoo, is an expert at following suspects. The element of surprise works in his favor: No one expects a bird to be a detective!

You can help Lily, David, and Josh solve the mysteries in this book. Just read the stories, and try to answer the questions. Here's a hint: Look at the pictures for clues!

CLUE ONE: The Sugar Shack Is Closed! It's Summer Vacation!

Lily, David, and Josh gave their headquarters one last look. No, they hadn't left anything behind. With the exception of the rickety old table they used as a desk, the Sugar Shack was empty.

All of the shelves in the store had been cleared. Before closing up, Frank had poured all of the leftover candy from the jars in the window into big paper bags. It was his annual gift to the residents of Seahorse Cottages, the beach community in Seaside, where the gang vacationed each summer.

After saying a final good-bye to the Sugar Shack, Josh, David, and Lily jumped on their bikes. Their destination: Ravenhill Manor, Lily's grandfather's luxurious home at Seahorse Cottages. He had invited the detectives to stay with him for a few days. Lily's uncles, Frank and Tony, planned to join the kids later. Squawking happily, Robinson led the way as the detectives pedaled behind him.

Several miles outside of town, the group turned onto a sandy road that made pedaling their bikes really difficult. When they arrived at a fork in the road a few minutes later, they decided to stop and take a break. Josh wiped the sweat from his forehead while Lily scratched her head in confusion. Right or left at the fork? She couldn't remember. And the road's old sign, knocked down years ago by the wind, wasn't any help. It was David who finally figured out which way to go. He pointed at the correct path and told Josh and Lily, "Since Lily's grandfather always brings the eggs from his farm to the village in his truck, it must be this one!"

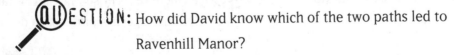

QUESTION: How did David know which of the two paths led to Ravenhill Manor?

CLUE TWO: Halt! Who Spies There?

After years of having a truck drive over it, the grass on the right path refused to grow—that must be the right way! After half an hour of hard pedaling, Lily and her friends finally made it to the front door of the house.

"Welcome to Ravenhill Manor!" Lily's smiling grandfather said as he opened the front door. "I hope everyone got good grades this year because if not, it's dish duty for you!"

"I'm not worried," Lily said with a laugh. She was proud of the straight As on her last report card. "And even if I was, I think I'd be able to handle pressing the 'on' switch on the dishwasher."

Her grandfather chuckled. "Come on, Josh and David, let's take a tour of the house to work up our appetites."

Later that afternoon, Frank's red motorcycle pulled into the driveway. Tony and Frank lugged their suitcases into the house. "Before you settle into your rooms, come drink a glass of the hot cider I just whipped up. I want to hear all of your news," Lily's grandfather told Frank and Tony.

"Great idea," said Frank as Josh, David, and Lily settled next to him. "But where did Robinson fly off to?"

"He found a perch to spy on us from," replied David.

"And I have a feeling he's not the only one," added Lily. "Someone's been watching us for a while now."

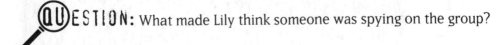

QUESTION: What made Lily think someone was spying on the group?

CLUE THREE: Under High Surveillance

"That was weird," David said the next morning at breakfast between bites of toast.

"Completely suspicious!" Lily agreed. "Whoever was spying on us yesterday from the dormer window of the tower must have been up to something. Maybe we should climb up there to look for clues."

After breakfast, the detectives stood in the courtyard trying to figure out the best way to get into the tower. As they were debating, Robinson flew overhead and dropped something shiny on the ground. It was a gold coin!

"This coin looks old," said Lily. "Just like the ones in Grandfather's collection."

The detectives found Lily's grandfather in the library with Frank and Tony. The kids eagerly showed him the coin that they found. He scrutinized it with the eye of a true collector, then walked up to the glass case that proudly displayed his *own* coin collection.

"Baffling!" he murmured to himself. "The Empress Veronica. I have a coin in my collection that looks just like it, but it's supposed to be one of a kind. Here, check it out."

Grandfather placed the two coins side by side. Tony flipped them over to examine them.

"Same stamp," Tony concluded. "But that's what makes the coin unique. How could there be two coins with the same stamp?"

"May I have a look?" Josh asked. He turned the coins over and studied them carefully, checking for any differences between the two.

Suddenly, he gasped. "Lily's grandfather's coin is authentic. The other is definitely a fake!"

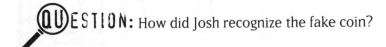 QUESTION: How did Josh recognize the fake coin?

Fake Coin   Original

CLUE FOUR: Where There's Smoke, There's Fire

It was the Empress's earring that gave the counterfeit away.

Later that night, the detectives gathered in the boys' bedroom to discuss the case. Together, they flipped through a book about ancient coins that they found in the mansion's well-stocked library. Finally, David found the page they had been looking for. He read aloud: "'The Empress Veronica: a very valuable coin, only twelve of which were minted in Venice in 1634. The boat that was supposed to transport the twelve coins to their owner was lost off the coast of Gibraltar. Only one coin was recovered and later returned to its owner, Prince Hernando Aranjuez. After his death, the prince left the coin to his oldest son, who used it to pay for the dowry of his daughter. After passing from owner to owner, the coin eventually entered into a private collection.'"

Josh yawned. "Bo-ring! That doesn't help us at all. What we really need to know is where the fake coin came from."

"Well, it couldn't have been outside for very long or it would look weathered," Lily concluded.

"Which means that whoever counterfeited the coin might not be too far from here," David proposed.

The clock struck midnight as the detectives tiptoed down the stairs to put the book back. Every step they took down the stairs made a loud creaking sound.

"We must be the only ones awake," Lily whispered, a little spooked.

"No, I don't think so," Josh replied. "Someone just left here. I can feel it. And look! There's proof."

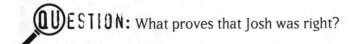 **QUESTION:** What proves that Josh was right?

CLUE FIVE: What Nerve!

If the stranger had snuffed the candle instead of blowing it out, the detectives wouldn't have been able to see or smell its smoke.

The next morning, at exactly 7:13 A.M., a frightening cry cut through the silence of the house. David immediately jumped out of bed and ran into Lily in the hallway; she had also hurried out of her room. They woke Josh up and then ran toward the direction of the voices coming from the parlor. They learned that the library window had been broken during the night, and now the Empress Veronica was missing! The detectives quietly let themselves into the library and approached the coin case.

Suddenly, Josh jumped. He had stepped on something! He bent down to examine the object: It was an ordinary gray button. He hid the button in his pocket, reminding himself that *anything* could be a clue.

In the parlor, the excitement was mounting. Elsa, the mansion's cook, was a wreck: She was the one who had discovered the burglary. Grandfather sat gloomily in his favorite armchair while Frank and Tony interrogated the staff.

"What nerve!" Lily murmured. "The stranger must have stolen the coin during the night."

"Stranger?" David asked. He had a look in his eye that meant he knew something the others didn't. "The thief is right here in this room."

QUESTION: How did David know who the thief was?

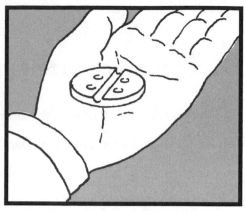

CLUE SIX: You May Not Have Noticed . . .

If he had realized that he was missing a button on his vest, Albert Douglas would surely have gone to change before appearing in the parlor. The three detectives watched him from the corner as he talked to the young gardener in overalls.

"It's horrible!" they heard him say. "I hope the police find the thief."

"So do we," Lily murmured to Josh and David. "And we're going to help them. Poor Grandfather! He hired Douglas as a chauffeur three months ago because he seemed so kind and hardworking. But he can't fool us!"

"Calm down, Lily," said Josh. "Other than the button, we don't have any proof."

But Lily had already slipped out of the parlor. Her friends followed and joined her in front of Albert Douglas's door.

"Locked!" she said, raising an eyebrow. "Hmm. That says a lot about his personality."

"Not really," David countered. "Everyone has a right to privacy."

Josh let his friends talk. With one eye to the keyhole, he murmured, "You're going to have a hard time finding clues in this room, Lily. There's nothing interesting in here."

"I disagree!" Lily cried after taking a look through the keyhole herself.

"What are you doing here, you scoundrels?" growled Albert Douglas, who suddenly appeared from around the corner.

"I . . . um . . . uh . . . I was visiting the house. And I got lost!" Lily lied.

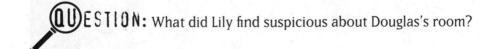 **QUESTION:** What did Lily find suspicious about Douglas's room?

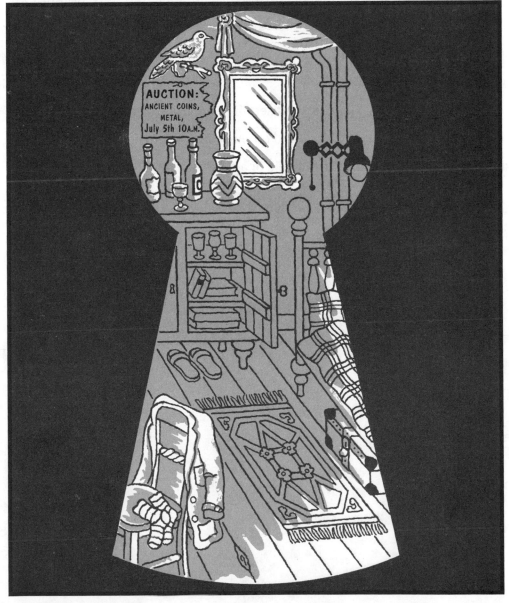

AUCTION:
ANCIENT COINS,
METAL,
July 5th 10 A.M.

CLUE SEVEN: So It Goes

Douglas had a poster announcing an ancient coin sale hanging on his wall!

Frank listened, bewildered, to Lily's story while Tony took control of the situation. This was serious business. Tony decided to follow the suspect. He was a police investigator, and he knew he had to protect Lily and her friends. After all, they were the ones who had put Tony on Douglas's trail. If Douglas found out, he would surely want revenge. Tony needed to be as careful as possible. He exchanged a few words with his brother, who shared his opinion of the situation.

The next morning, the detectives set off in the truck with Frank at the wheel. They were headed to the beach. Tony followed on the motorcycle. The group met up again in the main room at Villanova Hall, in the middle of a huge auction.

"After we auction these tables, we will move on to a very rare coin," the auctioneer announced proudly.

"I don't see Douglas anywhere," Lily whispered, suddenly nervous.

"Me neither," said David. "That's a shame. We must have made a mistake."

"No," replied Josh, tugging on David's sleeve. "He's here. And he's not alone."

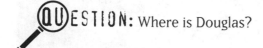 **QUESTION:** Where is Douglas?

CLUE EIGHT: A Policeman Who's Not Afraid of the Rain

Once David and Lily saw the chauffeur standing next to the exit, they quietly alerted Frank and Tony. Then they turned back to the auctioneer.

"Your attention, please, ladies and gentlemen! I now present to you a coin unlike any other in the world: the incomparable Empress Veronica!"

The auctioneer's assistant walked through the audience, showing the shiny coin to interested buyers.

Suddenly, Douglas spotted Frank and Tony. Dragging his friend by his arm, Douglas raced out of the room. The auctioneer watched, confused, as Tony, Frank, Lily, David, and Josh ran toward the emergency exit and out into the street. Through the pouring rain, the detectives could faintly make out two silhouettes sprinting toward the Traveler's Inn.

The group followed them, and five minutes later, Tony knocked on the door of room 17 in the Traveler's Inn.

"Police, open up! We know you're in there!"

"So come in, then," replied a low, sardonic voice.

"What a surprise!" Tony said sarcastically as he entered the room. There, lying in bed, was a man with a big mustache. "Fred the Forger! Have you gone back into business? That will cost you dearly."

"What do you want from me?" asked the man with the mustache. "I am a very sick man. I haven't left my bed for two days."

"I doubt *that*!" Tony replied.

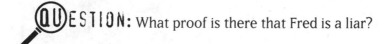 **QUESTION:** What proof is there that Fred is a liar?

CLUE NINE: Emergency Exit

Fred had put his wet umbrella in the umbrella stand by the window. It proved that he had been outside in the rain with Douglas.

"Get dressed," Tony told him. "I'm bringing you down to the station. As for your friend Albert Douglas, I'll take care of *him* later."

While Tony called for backup, the three detectives put all their clues together to solve the case.

"Fred and Albert learned that my grandfather owned the Empress," Lily said. "Fred made a fake coin that Albert must have tried to substitute for the original, which they hoped to sell at the auction."

"Except Douglas lost the forged coin, which Robinson found. Fred got mad and threatened his accomplice," David continued.

"And the accomplice didn't hesitate to break the window and steal the original," Josh said.

"He didn't have a choice," Lily remarked. "Grandfather always locks the case and carries the key with him. Wait, what's that?"

Lily walked up to the open window. Had Douglas snuck away down the fire escape? The friends studied the flower-filled courtyard.

"He's completely gone," said Tony, reading Lily's mind. "But don't worry, I know how to find him."

"It's okay, I've already found him!" Lily said. "Get ready, boys. Douglas is as good as arrested."

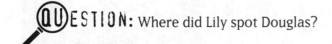 **QUESTION:** Where did Lily spot Douglas?

CLUE ONE: Three Departures, One Arrival

On Sunday night, Frank and Tony drove the three detectives to the train station. The night train was going to take them to Quebec, where they were going to spend a week to take a break from mystery-solving.

Josh, David, and Lily checked that their tickets, their passports, and the letters from their parents giving them permission to leave the United States were all where they should be. The train was right on time, and soon the three friends were hurtling through the darkness toward Canada.

The detectives passed the time on the train by going over the events of the past few days, which had culminated in Douglas's arrest.

"I'll never forget the look on his face when we pulled the lid off of that garbage can he was hiding in!" Lily laughed.

"He had no idea what was going on," Josh agreed.

"It seemed like it took him a while to realize what had happened, even when he was in prison," Lily added. "What do you think, David?"

David didn't answer; he was fast asleep with Robinson tucked under his ear.

Meanwhile, back in the train station, Tony was busy studying the arrivals board. He was hot on the trail of a jewel smuggler. According to his sources, the suspect came into town regularly from Toronto.

"He's not going to arrive tonight," Frank declared.

"You're wrong. In fact, we have just enough time for a cup of coffee," Tony told him.

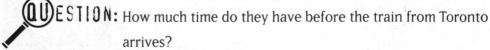 **QUESTION:** How much time do they have before the train from Toronto arrives?

TRAIN NO.	SCHEDULE	ARRIVES	TRACK	ARRIVING FROM
NE 321	SAT & SUN	4:39 P.M.	2	TORONTO
NIA 4589	MON THRU FRI	5:02 P.M.	5	ALBANY
BOS 555	EVERY DAY	5:50 P.M.	1	POTSDAM
NIA 4588	MON THRU FRI	6:19 P.M.	6	FISHKILL
BOS 555	EVERY DAY	6:50 P.M.	1	POTSDAM
NE 258	SAT & SUN	6:51 P.M.	1	RHINEBECK
NE 322	EVERY DAY	7:10 P.M.	1	WORCESTER
NIA 4590	MON THRU FRI	7:18 P.M.	5	ALBANY
WAS 4573	SUN & HOLIDAYS	7:23 P.M.	5	ALBANY
NE 657	EVERY DAY	7:43 P.M.	2	UTICA
BOS 501	EVERY DAY X SUN	7:50 P.M.	1	POTSDAM
NE 651	MON THRU FRI	7:58 P.M.	2	TORONTO
NE 647	EVERY DAY	8:13 P.M.	2	NIAGA
NIA 2369	EVERY DAY	8:29 P.M.	6	BOSTON
NIA 3258	EVERY DAY	8:31 P.M.	5	NEW YO
BOS 522	MON THRU SAT	8:43 P.M.	4	SARATO
NE 333	SAT & SUN	8:55 P.M.	3	MONTREAL
NE 777	EVERY DAY X MON	8:57 P.M.	2	SYRACU
NIA 4598	MON THRU SUN	9:40 P.M.	5	TORO

CLUE TWO: A Shadow in the Night

Despite the late hour, the train station was still bustling. Frank looked at his watch. Tony was right. They had exactly thirty-five minutes before the train from Toronto arrived.

They chose a café to sit down in where they could survey all of the comings and goings in the station. The brothers took their time enjoying two cups of coffee. The waiter had just cleared their table when, suddenly, they saw a figure in black emerge from a train carrying a suitcase. Hidden in the shadows, the man tiptoed across the platform.

"That's our man," murmured Tony. "He's hurrying away, and he seems really nervous."

"If that's really him," said Frank, "his accomplices must have warned him that we would be here."

Just then, a headlight from a train entering the station fully lit the man's face. Tony grabbed his brother's arm. "That's him, all right! And he's ours! Two against one, he has no chance!"

Tony jumped up from the table to try to run after the suspect, but he stumbled and fell. The man with the suitcase disappeared from sight.

"Don't worry about it," Frank reassured him. "I still see him."

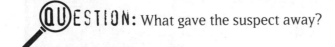 **QUESTION:** What gave the suspect away?

CLUE THREE: From One Hand to Another

After storing his suitcase in compartment 12 of the station locker room, the man with the black eye patch put his key in his pocket and walked toward the exit. Tony and Frank followed him.

The man confidently walked toward the North Star, a large café across the street from the train station. The two brothers followed him inside and sat down at a table near the back of the restaurant.

Frank and Tony watched as the man placed the key on the food counter. The waiter approached the man to take his order. The waiter slid a glass of soda across the counter to the man, and he sipped it calmly. All around, customers were talking and having a good time. The clock ticked by slowly. Frank was getting impatient.

"Tony, if you want my opinion, we're wasting our time. Your suspect is already on his second glass of soda, and nothing out of the ordinary has happened. He seems more like a harmless old man than a hardened jewel smuggler."

At that moment, a group of people passed in front of Frank and Tony's table, obstructing their view of the counter for a split second. When the group moved, Tony and Frank saw that the man, and the key, had disappeared!

"He must have snuck away with the key!" cried Tony, ready to run. But Frank held his arm.

"Maybe, but he doesn't have the key, because I know who does. Quick! Follow me!"

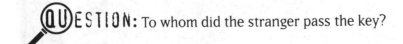

QUESTION: To whom did the stranger pass the key?

CLUE FOUR: Pseudonym

The man with the black eye patch had, in fact, planned a date at the café! His date was a woman who, after secretly collecting the locker key, fled from the café.

After picking up her suitcase from the curb, she climbed into a taxi and sped away. Frank and Tony jumped in another cab and followed the woman.

Soon, Frank and Tony found themselves in a dirty area on the outskirts of town, where the woman slipped out of the cab and disappeared behind the basement door of a house. Tony and Frank paid their fare and rushed out to inspect the house. The sign on the wall of the house read INGRID CROCKERY. Nothing moved behind the nearby small, dimly lit window.

Even though they knew it was dangerous, the two brothers decided to have a look around. They saw that a narrow alleyway led to the back of the house.

Frank and Tony peered into a window and watched as the woman hastily scrawled a few words on a piece of paper. She loaded the paper into a fax machine. The sheet of paper disappeared through the top of the machine and slid back out into a tray in the bottom. From there, Tony was able to read the message on the piece of paper.

"Mona Sidd?" Tony asked his brother, surprised. "I thought her name was Ingrid Crockery."

After a few moments, Frank declared confidently, "Mona Sidd is actually an anagram—you have to scramble the letters to understand the message!"

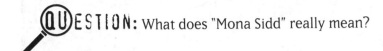

QUESTION: What does "Mona Sidd" really mean?

CLUE FIVE: Distraction

Ingrid Crockery was sneaky! When the letters of Mona Sidd were rearranged, they spelled out the word *diamonds.*

Frank was right! Tony complimented him. "Congratulations! You're turning into a bona fide detective after all! Now all we have to do is find out what "Yellow Dragon" means. It must be important because she wrote it down on the piece of paper. A cabaret? A restaurant? A nightclub?"

The two brothers spent the rest of the night drinking coffee and doing research in Tony's office. They looked in the telephone book and browsed the Internet. There was no sign of a Yellow Dragon!

It was well after midnight when, to get his mind off of his work, Frank opened the newspaper to the town's weekend event schedule. Maybe they could go to a show? He and Tony definitely needed to get their minds off the case for a while. Frank quickly glanced over the page and started to shut the newspaper after he couldn't find anything that sparked his interest.

"Not so fast!" Tony exclaimed, peering over his brother's shoulder. "The location of the meeting place is crystal clear. All you have to do is read!"

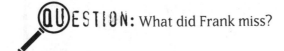 QUESTION: What did Frank miss?

OUTING IDEAS FOR THE WEEKEND

OUTDOOR THEATER: MARTIANS ARE COMING. An astounding show! Saturday and Sunday at 9.

SAFARI PARK: PICNIC WITH THE PANTHERS! EVERY DAY AT 1:00. Free for children under 6.

THE GREAT POTATO SACK RACE; BEGINS IN FRONT OF TOWN HALL AT 10:00. PRIZES AWARDED.

SUMMERFEST: FLAMENCO GUITAR CONCERT 7P.M. VIOLINS SUNDAY, 7P.M.

CAKE WALK: SAT. 6P.M. EAT TILL YOU DROP!

DIGITHON: GAMMA BYTE SUNDAY 3P.M. ARTISTS

PM

COLIBRI THEATER: "WHEN THE NIGHTINGALE SINGS" FAMOUS FOLKSONGS PERFORMED BY THE COMMUNAL CHOIR 7:30P.M.; SUNDAY MATINEE 3P.M.

DARK THEATER: A BLACK NIGHT IN BRISTOL. 12 years and older. 8P.M. Saturday and Sunday. Additional show at 11P.M.

PALACE OF THE GIANTS: MONSTER PARADE AND COSTUME PARTY! COME, ONE AND ALL, IN YOUR SCARY BEST!

LIGHTWEIGHT CHAMPIONSHIPS SATURDAY 10A.M.: the second round of eliminations in the Hillsdale Cup.

CANOE RACE ON ROSE LAKE: SIGN UP AT TOWN HALL. BEGINS SUNDAY AT 2P.M.

LAUGHTER AND FUN! 25TH ANNUAL CARNIVAL! MERRY-GO-ROUND, FERRIS WHEEL, ATTRACTIONS FOR THE YOUNG AND OLD! THE MONKEY MAN, THE SNAKE LADY, AND THE YELLOW DRAGON. FIREWORKS display. LOVE TUNNEL, FAIRGROUNDS, STARTING FRIDAY. FESTIVAL MEETING

MUNICIPAL LIBRARY

TREASURE HUNT: organized with the cooperation Municipal. Meet at Square.

AMERICANRAP EXPRESS: FINALISTS! PUBLIC CONCERT TRAIN STATION ON SATURDAY, STARTING AT

WEST OF THE MISSOURI: a unique version of this American classic. Sunday 7P.M. (4 hours long.)

DO YOU BELIEVE IN GHOSTS? GHOST PARTY. SUNDAY AFTER MIDNIGHT. COSTUMES PROVIDED.

MESSENGER PIGEONS! A DISPLAY OF COME BACK!

CLUE SIX: Looking for the Little Monster

The Yellow Dragon was the name of a stand at the yearly carnival that took place in a field right outside town. The next night, well before the time written on the fax message, the two brothers stationed themselves close to the carnival's entrance.

"Ingrid Crockery! What a surprise!" Frank murmured when he saw her appear a few minutes later.

"Don't get too excited. It's a carnival," Tony told his brother. "See, she's only selling lottery tickets for a chance to win one of those stuffed animals."

"You don't get it, do you?" Frank retorted. "Imagine if the diamonds are packed *inside* one of those innocent stuffed animals. Then the exchange could take place right in plain view!"

The irresistible scent of grilled sausages floated through the air. Frank's and Tony's stomachs grumbled; they hadn't had time to eat dinner today. It was five minutes to eight—just enough time to grab a snack at a nearby sausage stand before the eight o'clock meeting time written on the message. When Frank and Tony returned to the Yellow Dragon, a quick glance was enough to let them know that they had missed the eight o'clock drop-off. Inspector Tony was furious.

"You were right about those stuffed animals," he said to his brother. "Someone ran off with the whole stash while we were gone. Now we have to start looking for clues all over again."

"No, you're wrong," Frank told him. "If we hurry, we can catch the lucky winner. He didn't get far."

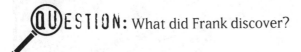 **QUESTION:** What did Frank discover?

CLUE SEVEN: The Elephant Man

A man carrying a stuffed elephant passed in front of the balloon stand. Frank and Tony immediately took off after him.

They followed the man outside the carnival's grounds, hiding and ducking behind trees and bushes. A few minutes later, the man arrived at an ivy-covered house. He stood at the front door and made sure the coast was clear. When the man was confident that he hadn't been followed, he let himself inside the house and shut the door. Seconds later, Tony leaped from his hiding place and rang the doorbell. Silence. Tony rang again. Nothing! Just as he was about to ring the bell a third time, the door opened partway.

"Police!" ordered Tony. "It was you who won a stuffed elephant at the carnival, right?"

"I think you are mistaken, sir, but come in anyway! I was just watching the soccer match on TV. It's two to one. What suspense!"

"Yeah, soccer match," Frank murmured to himself. He had just spotted the stuffed elephant crammed into the recycling bin. "You forgot to take off your coat," Frank said sarcastically.

"I am sensitive to the cold, sir," the man replied quickly.

"That's nonsense!" Tony exploded. "I'm going to arrest you for diamond smuggling! Here's the proof!"

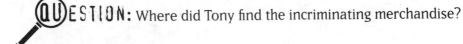 **QUESTION:** Where did Tony find the incriminating merchandise?

YELLOW
DRAGON
DIAMONDS

CLUE ONE: The First Trail

Dear friends and associates, Canada is a little chilly but really fun. We miss you! Love, Lily, David, and Josh.

P.S.: Thanks for your e-mail and congratulations! Finding the infamous Yellow Dragon diamonds in a pot under the staircase? What a feat!

Tony was closing the files on the case of the Yellow Dragon at his office when the postcard from the detectives arrived in the mail. He was reading it over with a smile on his face when the phone rang. Tony picked it up and heard a voice trembling with rage on the other end of the line. "This is Bruno Tompkins, the head of security at the Museum of Asian Art. It's incredible! Unheard of! Unseen! It all happened so fast . . . I had just made my rounds . . . Come quickly!"

At the crime scene, Tony and Frank found a very upset security guard. The guard told them, "At precisely 3:58 I heard a noise, like glass shattering, in the Hall of Indian Artifacts. I quickly sounded the alarm, but it was too late! Our greatest masterpiece, our most valuable statue, the Blue Madras, had vanished from its pedestal!"

Tony examined the crime scene for any clues. "This job is definitely the work of a specialist," said Tony. "There's not the slightest trace of evidence."

"Not so fast," Frank interrupted.

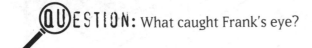 **QUESTION:** What caught Frank's eye?

INDIA
1696

CLUE TWO: As Plain as the Nose on Your Face

In his haste to escape, the thief had dropped his glasses. The inspector plucked them out of the case with the aid of a paper towel; he didn't want to smudge any fingerprints that might be on them.

In the museum lobby, the crowd of visitors was growing impatient. Since the discovery of the theft, all the exits had been sealed and monitored by security guards. While museum personnel patrolled the exhibits, the bathrooms, and the cafeteria, Tony, Frank, and Bruno Tompkins screened the service corridors and the cloakroom. Nothing.

At 4:25, a voice came on over the loudspeaker announcing that the museum was closing and all the visitors had to leave. The security guards made each visitor exit in a single-file line and show the contents of his or her bags on the way out. But nothing was found.

"Hmm. This makes me think that the thief got away with the statue before the guards sealed the exits," Frank said with a sigh.

"Look how thick the lenses of these glasses are. Our man must be really farsighted," Tony guessed, examining the evidence.

"Excellent point," Frank whispered excitedly in his brother's ear. "The man is still on the premises. Get ready to arrest him!"

 QUESTION: What alerted Frank to the thief's presence?

CLUE THREE: *Crack!*

Tony easily located the suspect, who was pretending to flip through a book but was actually holding it upside down!

Sensing that he was being watched, the man sprinted to the exit, squeezed past the security guards and exiting visitors, jumped down the stairs, and ran away. In his hands, he held the Blue Madras!

"Stop! Police!" cried Tony, running after the man.

But the thief paid no attention to Tony's orders and ran even faster. At the end of the street, there were two large trees that marked the entrance to the Public Gardens. The thief ran into the gardens and disappeared into the greenery.

Frank and Tony listened carefully for the sound of any branches snapping or bushes rustling, but other than the hollow pecking of a woodpecker, everything seemed perfectly calm. There wasn't even the sound of footsteps crunching on the gardens' gravel paths. After walking around every tree and peering under every bench, the two brothers had started pawing through the foliage of a massive rhododendron when, all of a sudden, they heard a strange noise.

"Come out, you're surrounded!" Tony ordered, rushing over to the place where he heard the noise come from. "And show us where you hid the statue!"

"Don't bother," Frank declared. "I just found it."

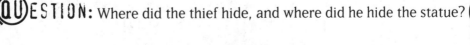**QUESTION:** Where did the thief hide, and where did he hide the statue?

CLUE ONE: A Noisy Entrance

"After hiding the statue in a bush near the gardens' fence, the thief climbed into a distant tree. Unfortunately for him, one of the tree's branches broke, which made a loud cracking noise . . ." Frank trailed off; he had been dictating a letter to Tony. The brothers were writing a letter to David, Lily, and Josh. Suddenly, a loud cry in the distance made Frank and Tony jump.

Through Tony's office window, they spotted Mrs. Lake, who lived across the street, waving her arms in the air. A few moments later, Frank and Tony were by her side.

"What a disaster!" she sobbed, showing the brothers her ransacked living room. "I left the house at noon to run some errands. When I came back half an hour later, the place looked like this!" Her voice trembled, and she started to sway like she was about to faint. Tony gently guided her over to the couch, while Frank examined the door that led onto her terrace.

"A classic move," Frank reported. "The thief broke one of the panes of glass so he could open the door from the inside."

Tony turned to Mrs. Lake and asked her, "Have you noticed any items that may be missing?"

"Oh, yes! The River of Diamonds, my beloved grandmother's necklace, and my late husband's pocket watch."

"Madam," Tony said with a smile. "I am happy to inform you that, in his hurry to get away, the thief forgot at least one of those two items."

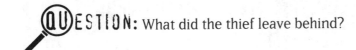 **QUESTION:** What did the thief leave behind?

CLUE TWO: Baby Steps

Mrs. Lake was overjoyed when Frank gave back her husband's watch, which he had found under the bureau! After thanking them repeatedly for helping her, she walked the two detectives to the gate. They promised to do everything they could to return her necklace.

After saying good-bye to Mrs. Lake, Frank and Tony discussed the difficulty of the case. They hadn't been able to find even the slightest hint of a trail in the old lady's house or garden.

Lost in his thoughts, Frank went to kick a few scraps of paper that were sitting on the curb with his toe, when his eyes suddenly widened. He quickly knelt down and began gathering the scraps of paper up and rearranging them.

"It's missing a piece," he said, still examining the pieces of paper, "but I think we're on the right track. What do you think?"

But his brother had already walked away toward a phone booth to flip through the phone book attached inside. He opened it to the page that showed a map of Hillsdale.

"This map can't be connected to the burglary," he said with a sigh. "There isn't a single street in all of Hillsdale that ends in *elands*."

"Curious," Frank murmured. "That sounds familiar."

"You're right!" Tony exclaimed after a few moments of studying the map of nearby Seaside, the gang's summer hangout. "There it is! It's in Seaside!"

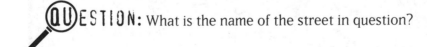 **QUESTION:** What is the name of the street in question?

Meet at
5 P.M.
5
lands
Street

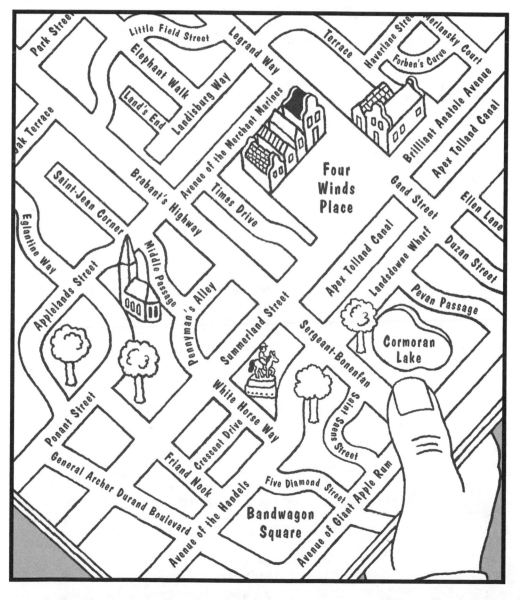

Park Street

Little Field Street

Legrand Way

Terrace

Haverlane Street

Merlansky Court

Forben's Curve

Elephant Walk

Landisburg Way

Land's End

Oak Terrace

Avenue of the Merchant Marines

Brilliant Anatole Avenue

Apex Tolland Canal

Brabant's Highway

Times Drive

Four
Winds
Place

Gand Street

Ellen Lane

Saint-Jean Corner

Eglantine Way

Applelands Street

Middle Passage

Pennyman's Alley

Apex Tolland Canal

Landsowne Wharf

Duzan Street

Pevan Passage

Summerland Street

Sergeant-Bonenfan

Cormoran
Lake

Ponant Street

White Horse Way

Crescent Drive

Saint Saens Street

Friand Nook

General Archer Durand Boulevard

Avenue of the Handels

Five Diamond Street

Bandwagon
Square

Avenue of Giant Apple Rum

CLUE THREE: Bric-a-Brac in Bulk

Tony and Frank parked their motorcycle in front of number 5 Appelands Street. The sign over the door of the store read MISCELLANEOUS MARVELS. Frank pushed the door open. A bell chimed, and a man emerged behind the counter, scrutinizing them. He looked unfriendly.

"Are you the owner of this store, Mr. . . . um . . ." Frank began.

"Martin, Marcus Martin. What can I do for you?"

"We would just like to ask you a few questions."

"At your service," Marcus Martin growled sarcastically.

"Well, we're looking for a diamond necklace—"

"I must stop you there," Marcus Martin interrupted. "I no longer sell any valuable jewelry. It's too expensive for vacationers; I couldn't sell any of it. What they want are affordable baubles, so I filled my shop with them instead, as you can see."

"We have a reliable source that says someone asked you to resell the River of Diamonds by this afternoon."

"Ridiculous!" cried Marcus Martin. "Why would I do something like that?"

"That's exactly what *we've* been wondering, sir. Why don't you and your accomplice tell us, since we know it's here? Don't bother denying it," Frank said.

QUESTION: How do Tony and Frank know that the River of Diamonds is in the shop and that Mr. Martin has an accomplice?

CLUE ONE: Someone Is Missing!

Mrs. Lake was ecstatic to have her River of Diamonds back. Marcus Martin had hidden it in the mouth of the stuffed antelope head on the wall of his store. Too bad that his accomplice, who was hiding behind a curtain in the store, got away before Tony and Frank could identify him.

Their last case was so easy to solve that Tony and Frank decided to reward themselves with a trip. They decided to go to the island of Seagull Cove, where they spent time during the summers when they were kids.

A crowd of squawking seagulls greeted the ferry as it pulled into the Kingston port at one o'clock. Over the ferry's loudspeaker, the captain informed the passengers that the boat would return to the mainland at four o'clock exactly and wished them a pleasant afternoon on the island.

The tourists spilled from the ferry and went off to shop, sunbathe, or enjoy a stroll. Frank and Tony decided to take a dive off Purgatory Point before having a delicious lunch at the Laughing Crab Inn. Afterward, they took a long walk along their favorite stretch of beach, made sand castles, and went fishing. After a fun and exciting day, they were the last passengers to board the ferry. Suddenly, the captain cried, "Stop everything! We're missing someone!"

"It's true," said Tony, counting the passengers. "But who?"

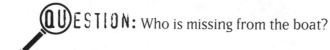 **QUESTION:** Who is missing from the boat?

CLUE TWO: Rescue

"Do you remember the woman who was sitting at the stern of the boat?" Frank asked.

"The one wearing a hat?"

"Yes. She was alone. I hope nothing happened!"

Frank and Tony decided to let the ferry leave without them and investigate. They described the lady to a passing hiker, who told them, "An elderly woman? Small, thin, wearing a big hat? I passed her on the path by the cliffs. We even said hello. She was going to visit Forban's Grotto by way of the chapel."

That was all Frank and Tony needed to hear! After half an hour of brisk walking, the two detectives made it to the chapel. It seemed empty; no one was nearby.

While Frank caught his breath, Tony walked ahead to the next turn in the path. He shielded his eyes from the glaring sun.

"Frank! Come quick! I think I found her!" he cried out in an alarmed voice.

Tony knelt before the woman, who was sprawled out on the pavement.

"She's still breathing," he said, relieved. Then his eyes darkened. "But she didn't faint on her own; she was drugged!"

"Well," said Frank, "it's clear that the scoundrel in question didn't skimp on the dose."

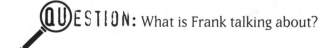 **QUESTION:** What is Frank talking about?

CLUE THREE: Settling Accounts

The woman's attacker had left behind a half-empty bottle of ether. The woman must have been forced to smell the ether, and then she fainted.

Tony and Frank gently tapped the woman's cheeks, speaking to her in soft voices. Slowly, the woman woke up. When she opened her eyes and saw the two men, she became alarmed.

"Don't be afraid," said Tony, introducing himself and Frank.

"What happened?" she asked, sobbing.

"That's what we'd like *you* to tell *us* so we can find whoever did this to you," said Frank. "Do you remember him at all?"

"No, everything happened so fast . . ." The woman trailed off, deep in thought. "Oh, wait! I remember something. He was tall and strong, and when he attacked me, I saw a tattoo of an anchor!" She straightened herself up, looked into her purse, and immediately went pale. "Good heavens! He took my wallet and all of my papers!"

"Don't worry. We'll get your things back, ma'am, and find the thief, too," said Tony. "Now, let us help you up."

The group slowly walked back to the harbor. When they made it back to the main square in Kingston, Tony whispered into Frank's ear, "Frank, look! There's the thief. Come on, let's have a word with him."

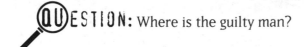 **QUESTION:** Where is the guilty man?

CLUE ONE: Vacation Souvenir

When they returned, David, Lily, and Josh heard all about Tony and Frank's latest adventure. The brothers had arrested the tattooed thief while he was calmly drinking a glass of wine at the Sea Spray Café.

A few days later, Lily set out to finish the roll of film in her camera so the detectives could develop the photos from their vacation.

Click! Lily snapped a photo of David and Robinson.

"Lily, forget the photos for a second and let's go get some ice cream!" David said.

Lily happily agreed. But on the way to the ice cream parlor, she took two more photos.

"Would you please stop?!" David griped.

"Okay, but there are only a few pictures left to take."

"Why don't you take them in the park?" Josh suggested.

Ice cream cones in their hands, the friends found a bench to sit on in the park. Lily finished her roll of film by taking pictures of birds building a nest nearby and ran off to develop it in the Sugar Shack's darkroom after finishing her chocolate cone. David and Josh met up with her back at the Sugar Shack a while later. Lily spread the photos out on the table for David and Josh to look at.

"Not bad," David admitted.

"You mean *great!*" Josh exclaimed. "Lily gives us a brand-new mystery to solve and all you can say is 'not bad'?"

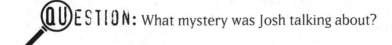 **QUESTION:** What mystery was Josh talking about?

CLUE TWO: A Prickly Thief

The last picture taken in the park showed, along with some pigeons perched on a fountain, a man in the process of stealing a lady's wallet from her pocket!

"It's a shame we can't see his whole face," David said.

"At least we know he has a beard," Lily commented, a little upset at herself for not perfectly photographing the thief.

"What if we enlarged the photo?" Josh suggested.

The first enlargement showed a small dark spot on the thief's collar. The second enlargement revealed that this little spot was actually a badge with the initials *CN*.

"That doesn't help us very much." Josh sighed. "There are thousands of people with those initials, from Cupcake Nevins to Chocolate Nicholson."

"I think Josh is hungry," David observed. "Maybe we should stop for dinner."

The next morning, the friends decided to go back to the park, hoping that the thief might revisit the site of his crime.

On their way there, Lily hurried to keep up with Josh and David, who were walking ahead. She was walking so fast that she almost tripped down a flight of stairs!

"Wait up!" she cried to David and Josh, who were far ahead; they were excited to get back to the park and start investigating. "My shoelace is unti—"

She broke off suddenly. "Wait! We don't need to go back to the park. I've found a trail!"

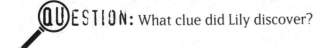 **QUESTION:** What clue did Lily discover?

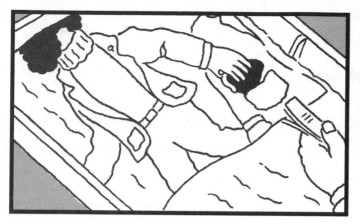

CLUE THREE: It Was a Little Boat . . .

"It's a good thing my shoelace was untied, because otherwise I wouldn't have noticed the insignia *CN*, for Club Nautilus," Lily explained to Josh and David once they ran back to see what was the matter.

"Ooh, let's go," David said dreamily. "I've always wanted to own a boat."

The detectives walked down to the docks and toward the club's shack. An old bearded man was stationed at the entrance, smoking a pipe.

"Wow," Lily murmured to David. "He looks *just like* a cartoon of a sailor."

"Hello, kids! How can I help you?" the man said cheerily.

"Hello, sir!" David replied. "We're looking for a man with brown hair and a beard. He offered to show us his boat today."

"Oh yes, of course! That would be . . . um . . . By all the winds! I've forgotten his name. I must say he doesn't come by very often. He was here yesterday, very briefly, to drop off a bag with a skull on it. It must be for a pirate party or something because—"

"Thank you!" Lily interrupted, sensing that the old sailor was about to start a story that might last for hours. They didn't have time to listen. They had a mystery to solve! "We'll come back another time."

The friends said good-bye and walked back to the docks, disappointed that they hadn't collected any valuable information. But as they were leaving, David noticed a clue that identified the thief's boat.

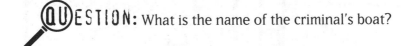 **QUESTION:** What is the name of the criminal's boat?

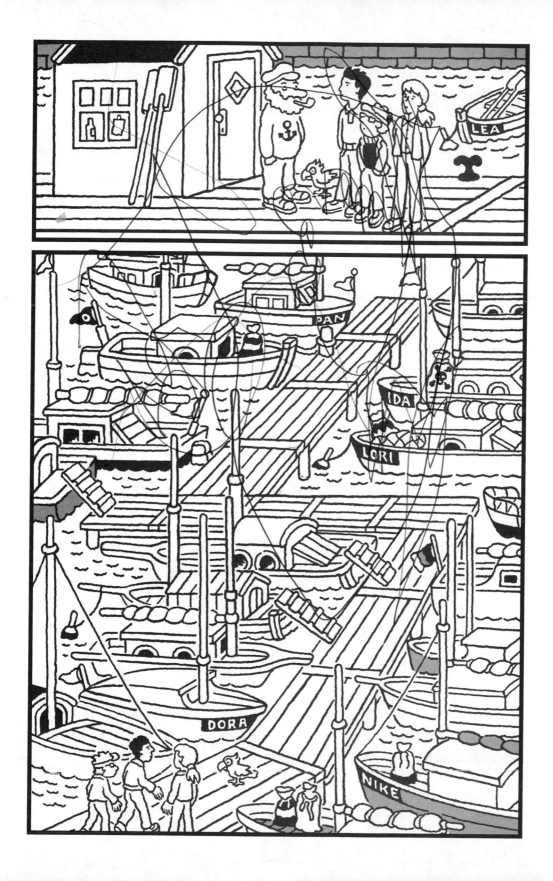

CLUE FOUR: Belowdecks

David had spotted the bag with a skull on it! The *Ida* was definitely the name of the thief's ship. The detectives walked to the boat. David and Lily jumped into the boat to look around while Josh and Robinson kept watch. Luckily, the pickpocket wasn't on the deck or in the cabin.

It was dark inside the cabin, so Lily had to light a lamp to hunt for clues. The two detectives found nothing of interest and were about to give up when David stumbled over a trapdoor hidden in the floorboards.

He opened the trapdoor carefully and stuck his head inside—a large sack was hidden inside the secret compartment! Lily held the flashlight while David inspected the sack's contents.

"Credit cards, IDs . . . we're on the right track," he murmured.

After a thorough inspection, David put the sack back in its place, closed the trapdoor, and went out to join Lily on the deck. She was explaining the situation to Josh, who was still keeping an eye out on the dock.

"What should we do now?" David asked. "We can't wait for him to come back; the old sailor said he doesn't come by very often."

"That doesn't matter," Josh proudly announced. "I'm certain we'll run into him soon, and I know where."

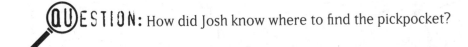

QUESTION: How did Josh know where to find the pickpocket?

FRIDAY:
PIRATE
BALL
AT CLUB
NAUTILUS

IDA

CLUE FIVE: The Pirate Ball

While Lily and David were busy searching the boat, Josh had discovered a flyer announcing a costume ball with a pirate theme the following Friday night at Club Nautilus.

On Friday night, the friends arrived at Club Nautilus with high hopes. They really wanted to catch the thief.

"I guess we should have worn costumes," Lily said when she saw everyone else at the ball.

"With Robinson on my shoulder, I don't need a costume," David joked.

"Can you see him?" Josh asked, his mind on the case.

"He's right over there," David replied. "And as long as he still has that dark beard, it will be easy to keep track of him all night."

The detectives split up and stationed themselves at different exits, hoping to keep track of the thief's movements while not attracting attention from the other partygoers. Josh was stationed closest to the club's main entrance, on the lookout for anything suspicious. It grew late, and the other partygoers started to leave, but the pickpocket seemed determined to stay until the end of the party.

The detectives were getting impatient.

Josh was especially tired of waiting around. He left his post at the party's entrance and snuck into the ball. Oh no! The thief was gone! He immediately notified Lily and David.

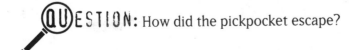 **QUESTION:** How did the pickpocket escape?

CLUE SIX: Chasing the *Seagull*

"We could have been waiting here forever," Josh commented. "It's a good thing I noticed him escaping on the canal!"

"Did you notice anything suspicious?" David asked anxiously.

"All I could see was the name of his boat: the *Seagull*."

The detectives took off into the night in search of the *Seagull*. It wasn't easy to find because it was completely dark out, and they were on foot, not in a boat. They crossed over one bridge after another, but the boat still drifted farther and farther away.

"Maybe the old sailor told him that we were looking for him, and now he's on to us," Lily remarked.

They stopped to take a breath in the middle of the next bridge and looked out into the canal for the boat. It had vanished!

"This time we've really lost him," David said angrily.

The detectives found themselves in a part of town that was filled with old grain warehouses. The only sounds they could hear at that hour were the gentle noise of the waves in the canal and the meowing of a few stray cats.

"This is unfair," Josh pouted.

Lily turned to look at him with a wild expression in her eyes. "I hope you boys aren't too out of breath," she exclaimed, starting to run again. "Because I just saw the *Seagull*! Come on!"

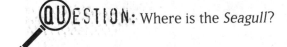 **QUESTION:** Where is the *Seagull*?

CLUE SEVEN: Noises in the Hallway

The *Seagull* was barely visible in front of the Tailor Brothers warehouse. The boat wasn't moving; the thief must have anchored it.

"Let's hurry!" David said, panting. "The thief must have already gotten off the boat."

The friends ran as fast as they could toward the *Seagull*. When they got there, they found out that it was empty. The sound of footsteps nearby made them jump.

"Quick, hide!" Lily whispered, pushing her friends into a shadowy doorway.

The thief passed by without noticing them and quickly walked toward a candy store on the next block. David took out his binoculars and watched him as he entered the store.

"I think our suspect has a weakness for peppermints," David said.

After buying a bag of candy, the burglar entered a dimly lit building next door. Very cautiously, the detectives followed the man to the landing on the first floor. They hid and listened in on a conversation between the thief and an old woman, who they guessed was his landlady.

"Here's my rent for the past month," said the bearded man. "I'm sorry for the delay, but money has been tight recently."

Lily scoffed, "What nerve!"

"Especially for a man with such varied resources," David added.

"What do you mean?" asked Josh.

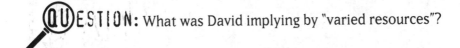

QUESTION: What was David implying by "varied resources"?

CLUE EIGHT: Off to Work!

Once they were outside, David explained to his friends: "Our friend must have really worked hard during the Pirate Ball. He took out a white wallet to pay for his peppermints and a black wallet to pay his landlady! That's what I meant when I said he had 'varied resources.'"

"What are we going to do to stop him?" Josh asked.

"He told his landlady to wake him up tomorrow at nine o'clock," Lily replied. "We should come back then with Frank and Tony."

The detectives rushed back to the Sugar Shack and called Frank and Tony to tell them about the mystery. Tony advised the detectives to wait until they caught the thief red-handed before they approached him.

The next morning, the detectives, along with Frank and Tony, stood watch in front of the robber's apartment building. The man left his apartment building at 9:30 sharp and proceeded to wander through the small alleyways hidden between the warehouses by the docks. Because they had to follow him at a distance, the detectives eventually lost sight of him at the bus station.

"He's as slippery as an eel," Lily lamented. "He wriggles through our fingers every time!"

"Let's think," Josh urged the others. "He can't be far off. There are tons of people here; it's an ideal place for a pickpocket."

"No, I think our bearded friend has other plans for the morning," David announced.

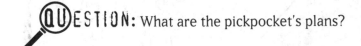 QUESTION: What are the pickpocket's plans?

CLUE NINE: The Beard!

Josh was right: Although the thief loved to work in crowded places, he wasn't interested in the bus station that morning. He was only there to catch the bus to Saint John's Cathedral in the center of town.

The detectives followed him in a taxi to the square in front of the cathedral and then continued to trail him on foot. The thief looked longingly at the nice cars parked around the square and the tourists carrying bulging purses and wallets. He searched the crowd for the easiest prey and finally settled on a group of retired couples on a guided tour. The tour guide launched into a long-winded speech about the life of Cardinal Florentine, and the thief took advantage of the opportunity by nabbing an old lady's purse.

"Thief!" the old woman cried out angrily.

After narrowly escaping being hit by an umbrella that belonged to one of the men in the group, the man sprinted away with the detectives on his heels.

"Stop him! Stop him!" Lily shouted, but no one reacted. The thief seemed to have escaped again.

Deeply discouraged because they thought they would never catch the thief, the detectives stopped for a breather in front of the door to the cathedral.

"He's too fast for us," David said, panting.

"Speak for yourself," Josh said. "I know that he passed by here and that he's probably inside the cathedral right now!"

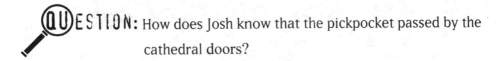

QUESTION: How does Josh know that the pickpocket passed by the cathedral doors?

CLUE TEN: A Matter of Conscience

Josh reached into a garbage can and pulled out a fake beard!

"He certainly fooled us," Lily admitted. "But not anymore! Good job, Josh!"

The detectives entered the cathedral, excited to be back on the case.

"He's going to be hard to spot without his beard," David whispered. "Plus, it's so dark and shadowy in here."

The detectives decided to split up so they could be sure to inspect every corner of the cathedral. David sent Robinson off to investigate and stationed himself near the exit. Lily inspected the organ, and Frank sat on a bench and pretended to look pensive. Josh examined the altar and the pulpit while Tony wandered through the pews.

After twenty minutes of searching with no result, the gang met up by the exit to discuss their next move. Everybody except Tony, who decided to have one last look around.

"I guess he didn't come in here after all," Frank concluded. "Or else we would have found him by now."

"I'm sorry to contradict you, my dear brother, but our thief is certainly here," Tony interrupted, striding up to the group with a grin on his face. "And this time, he won't be able to escape."

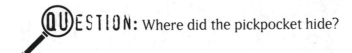 QUESTION: Where did the pickpocket hide?

CLUE ONE: A Curious Disappearance

The three detectives were standing in line to buy tickets for the morning's horse races. Lily passed the time by looking through the newspaper.

"Listen to this!" she announced, looking over the front-page story. "'Three young detectives successfully arrested a pickpocket hidden in a confessional at the local cathedral—'"

"Three tickets, please," David interrupted. He had finally made it to the front of the line.

The friends walked toward the racetrack. Josh stopped in front of the horses' stalls.

"Did you hear that?" he whispered.

Before Lily or David could ask what he meant, Josh pulled them behind the door of one of the stalls to listen in on a conversation between two men standing nearby.

"I don't understand how that could have happened," they heard a man say.

"They simply forced the bolt," the second man replied. "And what's strange is that he simply *let* them do it."

"If I don't find him before Saturday, I'll be ruined!" the first man said. "I've been counting on this victory!"

Aha! David thought. *This man's horse has been stolen.* "We should find out which horse he's talking about," David whispered to the group.

The three friends left their hiding place and walked around the stalls until Josh discovered which horse was missing.

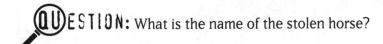**QUESTION:** What is the name of the stolen horse?

CLUE TWO: The Hunt for Clues

The only empty stall belonged to a horse named Apollo.

"What are you doing here?"

The three detectives jumped. The man they had heard earlier—the horse's owner—was striding toward them with an angry look on his face. David quickly introduced himself and his friends. Apollo's owner immediately became much more sympathetic.

"You're the famous detectives I was reading about in my morning paper! It's very nice to meet you. My name is Charles Rosenberg. Please excuse my disagreeable tone just now, but someone stole my horse last night."

"We know," Lily said.

"How do you know that? I just found out myself!"

"It's a professional secret," Josh said, smiling.

Mr. Rosenberg took a photo of a white horse out of his jacket pocket and proudly showed it to the detectives.

"Isn't Apollo a beautiful horse? Do you think you can help me find him?"

"We'll do our best," Lily replied confidently. "If it's all right with you, we'd like to start by inspecting his stall before anyone cleans it."

Mr. Rosenberg happily agreed. Josh, David, and Lily began searching through the straw with pitchforks. After a few minutes of searching, they were about to give up when David announced triumphantly, "You could say the thief left us a *pointed* clue . . ."

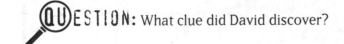 **QUESTION:** What clue did David discover?

CLUE THREE: At the Junkyard

"I am certain that it is an anesthetic," the veterinarian concluded after David showed him the syringe he found on the shelf in the horse's stall.

"That explains why Apollo was so easy to steal—he was sedated," Lily concluded.

Mr. Rosenberg called the police. As soon as they got there, they began collecting fingerprints.

Since there was nothing left for them to do inside the stall, the three detectives decided to ride their bicycles around the area to look for clues. After a few minutes of riding, they reached the main road and noticed that there were tire marks in a section of the road that had just been repaved.

"I bet these were made by the getaway car," said David. "The thieves were the only ones here last night after the parking lot was paved. In their rush to escape, they probably didn't notice that the pavement was still wet."

The three friends followed the tracks, which stopped only a few feet down the road. The group continued walking in the direction the tracks were headed. In a few minutes, they found themselves at Henry & Sons Junkyard.

"Maybe the thieves left their car here," Lily suggested. "Let's go take a look!"

Lily found the junkyard's owner, Mr. Henry, and started questioning him while David explored a mountain of old cars. Suddenly, Josh shouted out to his friends: He had found a vehicle that could be the one they were looking for!

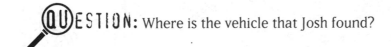 **QUESTION:** Where is the vehicle that Josh found?

CLUE FOUR: Bicycling

Josh saw a horse trailer behind a pile of old tires. But it couldn't be the right one because there wasn't any trace of tar on its tires. Deeply disappointed, the three detectives decided to go home and pick up the investigation again the next day after school.

After classes ended the next day, the detectives jumped onto their bicycles and rode to the area where they had lost the thieves' trail. They thoroughly inspected all of the streets in the neighborhood, but they *still* couldn't find a single piece of evidence. After a few hours, they decided to stop searching.

On the way home, Lily tried to change the subject of conversation.

"Did you know that Mrs. Michael's cat was rescued from that tree *again*?"

No one answered; Lily knew they were all still thinking about the case.

"The thieves couldn't possibly have disappeared into thin air!" David exclaimed.

"You're completely right," said Josh with a big smile.

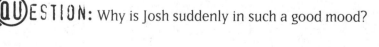**QUESTION:** Why is Josh suddenly in such a good mood?

CLUE FIVE: Deathly Silence at Number 9

Josh had spotted a saddle on the railing of number 9 Shrub Street. The detectives snuck up to the entrance of the house through a yard that looked like no one had cared for it in years. Robinson stood guard outside. It seemed like the house had been abandoned for a long time: There was garbage on the ground, and the plants all looked like they were dying.

"I'm going to knock on the door anyway," David decided. "You never know."

He climbed the stairs to the front door and searched for a name on the mailbox: no luck. He rang the doorbell, but no one answered. David tried again. There was still no response.

"Just give it up," Josh said as he kicked an empty soda can. "It's obvious that no one lives here anymore."

"You're right. Come on, Lily," David said. "Let's go."

Lost in thought, Lily didn't respond.

"Come on, Josh is right. You can see no one's here," David insisted.

"Are you sure?" Lily asked, a mischievous smile spreading across her face.

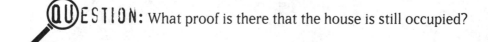

QUESTION: What proof is there that the house is still occupied?

CLUE SIX: All but One

Lily had noticed that the pendulum on the clock was still moving; someone must have wound it recently. After walking around the exterior of the house and deciding that no one was home at the moment, Lily and David slid inside through an open window and noiselessly climbed the stairs. They quietly searched the house.

David stopped his search for a moment and looked at Lily. What was the girl doing? "Lily! This is not the time to read the newspaper!" David exclaimed.

"It is, actually! Listen: 'Famous jockey Dillan arrested for drug use'! And guess who discovered the scandal?"

"Mr. Rosenberg?"

"Exactly. Dillan was getting revenge for—"

"Shhh!" David cut her off. He heard footsteps on the ground floor of the house.

"We've got to get out of here!"

They crept down the stairs as quietly as possible. The man who had come in was talking on the phone, but the two friends didn't stop to listen in to his conversation; they ran by when his back was turned and jumped back out the open window.

Once they were outside, they hurried over to where Josh was keeping watch. "Are you crazy? Why didn't you warn us that someone was coming?"

"What do you mean? I never saw anyone! And I never took my eyes off the front door and the window you went through."

"I think I know how he got in," David said suddenly.

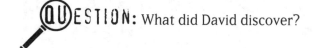 QUESTION: What did David discover?

CLUE SEVEN: A New Impasse

There was another entrance through the basement! The door next to the broom closet was open.

"Let's keep at it," David said on the walk home. "On the phone, I overheard Dillan ask for someone named Alfred Layton."

"Yeah, I heard that, too," Lily added. "He's meeting him in three days, on Wednesday, at ten o'clock. He was talking about payment for services rendered or something like that."

"Perfect! We can catch them at the same time," said Josh.

But first they needed to find Alfred Layton, which wouldn't be an easy job. They began the next day by consulting the phone book. There were seven people with the last name Layton, but only three of them had the first initial A.

Lily dialed the first number and asked to speak to Mr. Layton.

"Arthur? Are you there?" Lily heard a screeching voice cry out. "He's not here. Call back later."

There were only two more A. Laytons left on the list, but neither of them answered the phone. The detectives decided to visit them at home instead.

They started with the address that was closest to the Sugar Shack: 5 Sutton Street. When they arrived at the address, Josh sighed. "Wrong again! Someone named Layton lives here, but unfortunately, it's not the person we're looking for."

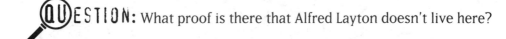 **QUESTION:** What proof is there that Alfred Layton doesn't live here?

CLUE EIGHT: The Truth About the Chickens

The address 5 Sutton Street was the home of Albert, not Alfred, Layton, as the sign in the window to the right of the door indicated.

It was too late in the day to visit the second address, so the friends decided to go the following day. Right after school ended, they grabbed their bikes and took off to visit the last Layton on their list, who lived just outside of town.

"There it is!" Josh exclaimed when they passed in front of an old, broken-down farmhouse. "It's not very pretty, is it?"

The three detectives left their bicycles behind a bush and walked toward the barn, hoping to find Apollo.

"Get off my land, you scamps!" they heard a voice call out. It was a man looking at them through a small window in the farmhouse. "You have no business here!"

Terrified, David started babbling excuses. Eventually, he explained that they were lost and just wanted to ask for directions back to town.

"Go left and keep heading straight. Now scram!"

"Wow, he's nice," Josh murmured sarcastically.

"Let's get out of here," said David. "There's nothing but chickens here anyway."

"Not exactly," Lily replied.

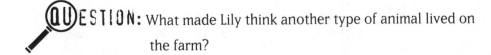

QUESTION: What made Lily think another type of animal lived on the farm?

CLUE NINE: Scoundrels in the Town Square

Lily's suspicions were confirmed by the hoofprints she spotted on Layton's lawn. After making sure the old man had left his post by the window, the detectives started investigating.

Behind one of the barn doors, they discovered a trailer used to transport horses. Josh looked at the tires and found tar!

Now all they had to do was find out where Layton and Dillan were meeting. Then they could catch them together and prove that they had stolen Apollo together.

"We can't follow Layton; he'll recognize us right away," Lily said.

"Robinson, we need you," David said to his cockatoo, who was perched happily on his shoulder. Robinson was pleased to be the center of attention.

Robinson took his duties very seriously. David rigged up a radar machine and attached it to Robinson's foot. It would allow the detectives to follow Layton by using the receptor in Tony's car.

The next day, Robinson set out after Layton's truck, followed at some distance by the detectives, Frank, and Tony in Tony's car. After half an hour on the road, they arrived at a crowded square, where Robinson flew back to join them. David was distressed.

"Oh no, Robinson! Why didn't you stay with Layton? How are we ever going to find him now?"

"It's okay," Lily reassured him. "I know where he is."

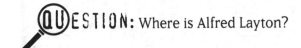 **QUESTION:** Where is Alfred Layton?

CLUE TEN: Look-alike

Layton and Dillan were in the middle of a conversation in an alley behind the Black Swan Inn. The group snuck up to them and tried to listen in on their conversation.

Distracted by a bowl of peanuts left on one of the tables in the inn, Robinson left his hiding place and flew too close to the crooks. Layton recognized him immediately.

"That's the cockatoo that belongs to those brats who were snooping around my place!"

"Let's separate," Dillan advised him. "Maybe they're on our trail."

The men split up. The detectives tried to follow them, but Dillan managed to lose them in the crowd. Instead, the detectives decided to follow Layton, who had returned to his truck. He drove away, and the detectives followed him at a safe distance. They were afraid they had lost him until they spotted a little dirt road that led to an abandoned shed.

They climbed out of the car and quietly snuck up to Layton's truck. He wasn't there!

All they found in the shed was a beautiful spotted horse and farming tools scattered around.

"It's a shame that isn't Apollo," said Lily, shaking her head.

"I think you're in for a happy surprise!" Josh said.

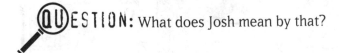 **QUESTION:** What does Josh mean by that?

CLUE ELEVEN: Caution, Wet Paint!

Josh rubbed his hand over the horse's coat to show that the spots had been recently painted! He figured out the trick once he spotted the poorly hidden can of paint.

"Layton must have been afraid that we'd find him, and he painted these spots on Apollo so we wouldn't recognize him," Lily said. "It's too bad we lost track of Layton."

"Okay! Hands up, everyone!" Alfred Layton suddenly stood up from where he was hiding in a haystack in the loft, a gun in his hand. "I'll teach you to meddle in other people's business!"

He started to climb down the ladder from the loft, his gun still pointed at the detectives.

Out of nowhere, Frank threw himself on the ladder. It wobbled, and Layton fell off the ladder and onto a small pile of straw on the ground. Tony quickly grabbed the gun, which had dropped out of Layton's hand during his fall, and pointed it back at him.

"The tables have turned, Mr. Layton. I'm arresting you for the theft of Mr. Rosenberg's horse."

"Horse? What horse? What are you talking about?"

"Don't play innocent, Mr. Layton. You know very well what I'm talking about! And I have proof!"

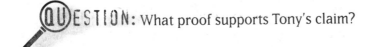 QUESTION: What proof supports Tony's claim?

CLUE TWELVE: Final Straw

When he realized that Tony had spotted the newspaper with information about the horse's theft lying on the pile of straw, Layton gave himself up without protest. Apollo returned to his stall. As for Dillan, he wasn't home when the police came to arrest him.

"Now there's a man who knows how to escape," David commented. "But we might have one more chance to catch him."

"How?" asked Josh.

"The horse race is tomorrow," Lily replied. "And I'm pretty sure Dillan will still do everything he can to keep Apollo from participating."

"You think he'd be crazy enough to go back to the stables?" David asked.

"Yeah, I do. I think he's ready to risk anything to get his revenge against Mr. Rosenberg."

The three detectives asked Mr. Rosenberg not to guard Apollo's stall that night, hoping to catch Dillan in the act. They hid behind a nearby building with a clear view of Apollo's stall. At 9:30 that night, they began to get impatient.

"I hope this plan works," Josh said between yawns.

"Shhh!!" David whispered. He had spotted a shadowy figure slip into Apollo's stall after breaking the padlock. The detectives raced into the stall, where they discovered Dillan in the middle of sabotaging the horse race!

 QUESTION: How was Dillan planning to keep Apollo from running in the race?

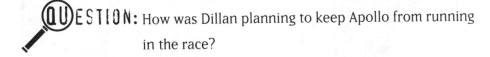

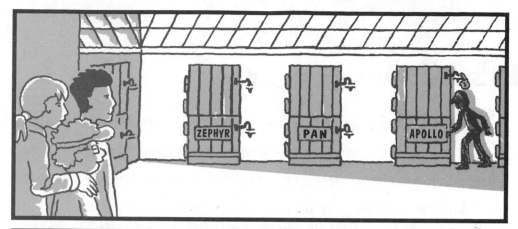

CLUE ONE: Carrot Ice Cream?

"I don't know what I would have done without you," Mr. Rosenberg said after Apollo won the race. "You really are first-rate detectives! When I think about Dillan trying to hurt Apollo by removing one of his horseshoes . . ." He shuddered. "Anyway, Dillan will have plenty of time to think about what he did while he's in prison."

But that wasn't the end of the mystery! During his interrogation, Dillan admitted that another horse's owner had paid him to make sure Apollo wouldn't win the race.

To celebrate another case closed, the detectives went to one of their favorite places for a victory dessert: the Ice Cream Palace. David ordered licorice ice cream for himself, bubblegum ice cream for Josh, and carrot sorbet for Lily, who had gone into the bathroom to wash her hands.

"If Lily doesn't hurry up, her dessert won't just be gross, it'll be melted, too," Josh said.

"Very funny," David said, feeding Robinson a nibble of his cone. "There she is."

"I'll bet you a second round of ice cream that I've found a new mystery for us! I overheard a very interesting conversation just now," Lily said excitedly.

"In the bathroom?"

"No, Josh, think about it," David replied.

 **QUESTION:** Where did Lily overhear this conversation?

CLUE TWO: Imprint

On her way to the bathroom, Lily had passed by a row of phone booths. Intrigued by the conversation being held by the woman in the middle booth, Lily pretended to talk into the phone in the next booth.

David and Josh wriggled with impatience. "Tell us!" they cried in unison.

Lily took a piece of paper out of her pocket with the notes she had taken in the phone booth. She read: "'Everything is finally ready . . . all the secret documents, as agreed . . . Try not to be followed.'"

"She made an appointment with the person she was talking to, but I couldn't hear when it was. She must have written it down here." She walked over to the middle booth and picked up the notepad sitting by the phone.

"How are you going to find out what she wrote?" David asked.

In response, Lily took a pencil and lightly colored over the entire top sheet of paper. Words appeared on the page as if by magic.

"'Alex, 6:15.' Do you think that's a code name?" Josh asked once they were outside the Palace.

"Not entirely," said David mysteriously.

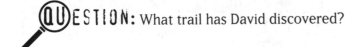 **QUESTION:** What trail has David discovered?

CLUE THREE: All Aboard!

As luck would have it, at the exact moment the three friends were discussing the meaning behind the name Alex, David spotted a sailor with the name written on the back of his shirt. Maybe Alex wasn't the name of the person the woman was talking to, but rather the name of the boat they were meeting on!

The detectives agreed to follow the sailor's trail. It took them all the way back to the port, where they walked up and down every dock, looking for the *Alex*. It was six o'clock when they finally found the ship they were looking for.

"Hurry! It looks abandoned! Let's get on the ship before anyone else does!" Josh said. Josh, David, and Lily pulled themselves up onto the deck of the ship.

"Not a soul in sight," David whispered, his voice a little shaky. "There's a light on in the cabin; maybe they're down there." He had barely finished his sentence when they heard footsteps on the deck.

"Everyone hide!" Lily ordered. They scrambled around, but it seemed like every possible hiding place was locked.

"Follow me, I found one!" Josh cried.

 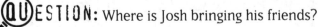 **QUESTION:** Where is Josh bringing his friends?

CLUE FOUR: A Coded Message

Josh led his friends over to the lifeboat. They climbed into it as quickly as they could and waited several long minutes for the footsteps to die away.

Once the deck was silent, the friends left the lifeboat. They tiptoed up to the lit window they had spotted earlier and peeked inside. They saw a man sitting in front of a computer, busily reading a message on the screen. From their hiding place, the three detectives could distinguish a series of letters, but they couldn't make any sense of it.

"We're out of luck." Lily sighed. "It's in code."

David took out a pencil and a piece of paper and copied the message. Just as he was done, the man turned off his computer and stood up from his desk.

Checking to make sure the coast was clear, the detectives jumped back onto the dock and immediately ran to the Sugar Shack, where they tried to decode the secret message. Two hours later, they still hadn't succeeded.

"There must be some logic to this text," said Josh, squinting at the letters. "We have to find the interval between the letters that serves as a break between words and the letters that form the real message."

"What a brainteaser!" David moaned. "Every time I think I've solved it, I realize I've forgotten letters!"

"I don't think so," Lily corrected him, smiling as she showed her friends the meaning behind the message.

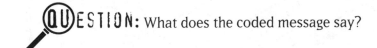 QUESTION: What does the coded message say?

CLUE FIVE: Document X

"What you have to do is start with the third letter and only read every third letter after that," Lily explained. "Then it reads, 'Operation Document X tomorrow night Ismanian consulate.'"

The following night, the three detectives met up at the Ismanian consulate. The gates were already closed. It would be too dangerous to climb over them, so they had to find another way to see what was going on inside.

Josh, David, and Lily walked around the building and found a tree with branches that grew close to the windows of the consulate. They all climbed into it. The view was perfect, but unfortunately, there wasn't much to see at the moment: The room was empty. The detectives had sat in the tree for forty-five long minutes, asking themselves what they were doing and wondering if they had made a huge mistake, when someone turned a light on inside.

It was a harmless-looking man with glasses. The detectives watched as he picked up a heavy-looking file and started to page through it quickly. Suddenly, he stopped searching and left the file open on the table. David, who was watching this scene through his binoculars, described it to his friends.

"He's taking out a pen—"

"He must want to copy the secret documents," Lily interrupted.

"No, he isn't writing anything down," David replied. "Wait—I think I know what he's doing."

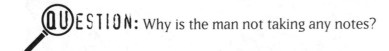 **QUESTION:** Why is the man not taking any notes?

CLUE SIX: An Obscure Problem

"Of course! Look at the way he's holding the pen," David exclaimed. "He doesn't need to take notes because his pen is also a camera!"

"With gadgets like that, he must be a secret agent. We're in the middle of a real mystery!" Lily cried.

The secret agent needed three different camera pens to copy the files. When he finished, he placed a bottle on the table and walked over to the door.

"It looks like he's going to grab a little snack," David reported.

Suddenly, the light in the room went out.

"What happened?" Josh and Lily asked.

"I don't know. I can't see anything."

The light came back on a moment later, and the spy reappeared.

"Maybe he turned out the light to take out the film without ruining it," Josh suggested.

"It looks like he's wrapping a present, but I don't see the film anywhere," David said. He thought for a moment, then continued, "There's only one place he could have hidden it."

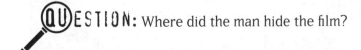 **QUESTION:** Where did the man hide the film?

CLUE SEVEN: Wrong Number

David noticed that the bottle on the desk had been opened and then carefully recorked. Seeing that the man was wrapping the bottle like a present, David deduced that it must be empty and must be where he hid the film! David's suspicions were confirmed when he saw the spy leave the consulate with the bottle in his hand.

The detectives left their post in the tree to follow the secret agent.

"Where did he go?" Lily asked when the group reached Station Street.

"There, in that phone booth," said Josh, gesturing discreetly.

They watched as the man dialed a phone number and hung up a few moments later, then dialed another number and hung up again. He looked around, then threw a piece of paper into a nearby garbage can and jumped into a taxi. He'd gotten away!

While Lily and David dug through the garbage, Josh went into the phone booth and pressed redial, hoping to find out what the last number the man dialed was.

"Oh no! It's information!"

David and Lily joined him in the phone booth a moment later, clutching the piece of paper that the spy had thrown into the garbage. It was a phone number! Josh dialed the number: 016 898 1080. Unfortunately, that number didn't exist.

"Wait," said Lily, who suddenly had an idea. "You dialed the number wrong, Josh."

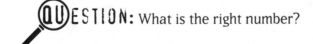 **QUESTION:** What is the right number?

CLUE EIGHT: A Night at the Opera

Josh was holding the paper upside down. All he had to do was turn it right-side up to see the correct number: 080 186 8910. Josh quickly dialed this number, which turned out to be the box office of a theater. When an operator answered, Josh asked what time the show would start.

"*The Masked Prince* will start at exactly 8:30, sir," the operator replied.

The detectives had seen posters around town for this show, which was playing at the Opera House.

"I wasn't sure what my plans were for tonight," Lily joked. "But now, let the show begin!"

Twenty minutes later, Josh, Lily, and David were walking around the lobby of the Opera House, looking for the spy. They couldn't find him. Eventually, they decided to take their seats and wait for any new clues to turn up. When they got to the ticket window, David thought he might have spotted him, but it was just a look-alike. The gang had to admit it: The spy had truly disappeared.

"Maybe he's already in the theater?" Lily proposed, unconvinced.

"Or maybe he's not coming at all," Josh muttered, discouraged.

"No, I can assure you he came through here," David announced triumphantly.

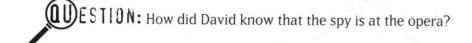 **QUESTION:** How did David know that the spy is at the opera?

CLUE NINE: Posted

Behind the woman at the ticket window, David had noticed a package wrapped in the same paper the spy used to wrap up the bottle with the film. This couldn't be a coincidence. When they got a little closer, they could read the card attached to the package: For V. K.

They decided to stay close to the ticket window to see who came to claim the package. It was a few minutes after the show began, and no one had arrived. They worried that the woman behind the desk might be in league with the spy, so they didn't dare ask her for information.

The detectives racked their brains. What was the connection between the spy in the Ismanian consulate and *The Masked Prince*? Nothing, as far as they could tell, but they weren't about to give up yet. Suddenly, a few latecomers burst in through the theater's doors, out of breath.

"Thank goodness we made it! Otherwise, we wouldn't have had an opportunity to see the show at all!" a young woman panted to her companion.

"That's it!" Lily exclaimed. "If tonight is the last night of the production, chances are that bottle is meant for one of the performers! Their next show is in another country, so they could smuggle the film!"

Now all the detectives had to do was find out which of the performers had the initials V. K.

"There it is! I found it!" cried Josh.

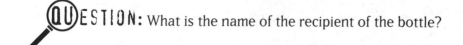 **QUESTION:** What is the name of the recipient of the bottle?

CLUE TEN: In the First Boxes

Josh had found a musician with the same initials as those on the card: the violinist Vera. Upon closer inspection, he discovered that her full name was Vera Kivivra.

The last bell rang, warning the audience that the show was about to start. The three detectives hurried to find their seats. They were seated in the second box, stage right. From their seats, they were able to watch the musicians as they finished tuning their instruments.

The conductor lifted his arms. The lights went down, and the audience's chatter died down into silence. Someone coughed.

The curtain rose, and the first overture began. While everyone else's eyes were on the stage, Josh studied the audience and the musicians through his binoculars.

"I think I've found the first violinist," he said after a moment. "But how can I know if she's actually Vera Kivivra?"

"Pass me the binoculars," Lily requested. She looked into the orchestra.

"Even if it's not Vera Kivivra, I can assure you that this is the woman who started it all."

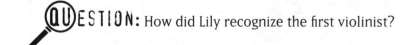

QUESTION: How did Lily recognize the first violinist?

CLUE ELEVEN: A Change in Decorations

Vera Kivivra, first violinist in the orchestra, was seated stage left, just in front of the singer. Her initials were written on her violin case. It was the same woman Lily had seen in the phone booth at the Ice Cream Palace! The clues were finally coming together!

During the last act, the detectives snuck back out to the ticket window and discovered that the package had disappeared!

Quickly, they ran to Vera Kivivra's dressing room. The door was unlocked, so they let themselves in. Vera wasn't there, so the detectives began to search for the bottle. They eventually found it hidden in a fold in the curtains.

When David opened the bottle, they saw that the film had been carefully hidden between little beads of lead to protect it from exposure. After sliding the film into his pocket, David carefully put all the lead beads back into the bottle. Once the bottle was safely back where they found it, the detectives quickly left the room.

The next day, the detectives asked to speak to the Ismanian ambassador about an urgent matter. He received them in his office, and they told him everything. After pausing for a few moments to think, the ambassador told them that the spy must be Victor Thornton, his personal secretary. But when he was accused, Thornton denied everything so calmly that the ambassador began to think that Lily, Josh, and David were playing a trick on him.

However, the spy had neglected to hide one very compromising detail . . .

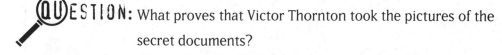

QUESTION: What proves that Victor Thornton took the pictures of the secret documents?

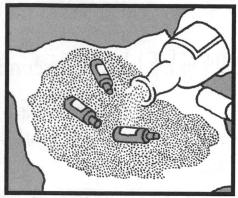

CLUE TWELVE: Crescendo

The ambassador congratulated the detectives warmly while the police arrested Victor Thornton. He had made the grave mistake of leaving his photo-pen in his desk drawer.

After they watched Thornton being led off to jail, Josh, Lily, David, Tony, and Frank met up in front of the opera. They asked the theater manager if they could speak to Vera Kivivra but were told that the orchestra had already left for the next stage of its tour. They leaped into Tony's car and sped off in hot pursuit of the musicians' van. The group caught up to them just as they reached the border. With the approval of the customs agents, Tony had all of the musicians' luggage unloaded. The bottle wasn't in Vera Kivivra's suitcase, and her violin case had mysteriously disappeared. She was outraged.

"This is unacceptable! You're treating us like common smugglers when we're musicians! You'll make us late with your ridiculous accusations, and we have a show to perform!"

Tony paid no attention to her and continued inspecting the luggage. Unfortunately, there was no sign of the bottle. Tony gave up his search, and the musicians started loading their luggage back into the van.

The detectives were confused. Where did the bottle go?

It was Josh who discovered it, just as the musicians were preparing to leave.

"You should have thought of another hiding place, Mrs. Kivivra," he cried.

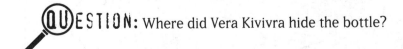 **QUESTION:** Where did Vera Kivivra hide the bottle?

CLUE THIRTEEN: A Well-Deserved Rest

Josh had spotted the violin case behind the bathroom door. Vera Kivivra had left it there right before the search and planned to retrieve it before the van left.

"My case! I don't understand how it got there!" she protested innocently.

The customs agents opened the case, and sure enough, there was the bottle!

"Uhhh . . . s-someone must be playing a t-trick on me!" Vera Kivivra stuttered.

The customs agent began to empty the bottle, and the violinist suddenly forgot her act. "But where is the fi—" she began, but stopped herself suddenly, realizing her mistake. It was too late!

"Fi? Do you mean film? What film?" Tony asked, pretending he didn't know anything. "Did this bottle contain film?"

"Yeah—I mean, no," the violinist replied cautiously.

The detectives were still laughing at Vera's mistake the next day, sitting in the ambassador's reception room. He was throwing a party in their honor. Convicted as an accomplice, Vera Kivivra would join Victor Thornton behind bars, while the detectives celebrated their most dangerous case yet.

But where was Robinson hiding? He had disappeared a few moments ago. The only thing left to figure out was where that cockatoo had flown off to . . .

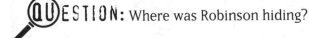 **QUESTION:** Where was Robinson hiding?

CLUE FOURTEEN: The Latest News

Robinson wasn't far off. He was enjoying the party in his own way: next to a delicious cherry cake! The detectives found the cockatoo at the buffet, sleeping like a baby, covered in whipped cream, and feeling very full.

That night, Josh, David, and Lily watched a summary on the news of their latest case. Thanks to their courage and insight, the spy ring had been dismantled! Even the man with the computer they had seen on the *Alex* was incarcerated. He was the head of the gang, involved in numerous cases and on the police's most-wanted list for years. Specializing in secret codes and false identities, he was extremely difficult to track. Little did he know that one day, Lily, Josh, and David would find him . . .